This book belongs to:

_____

Contents

Cover illustration by Russell Ayto
Illustrations on pages 32-33 by Peter Stevenson

A catalogue record for this book is available
from the British Library

Published by Ladybird Books Ltd
A subsidiary of the Penguin Group
A Pearson Company
© LADYBIRD BOOKS LTD MCMXCVII

A little too late!

written by Shirley Jackson
illustrated by Russell Ayto

Shopping
list
_____

bananas
potatoes
beans

A list,

Shopping
list

bananas
potatoes
beans

a bag,

a girl,

a house,

a bike,

a street,

a shop.

Birthday boy

written by Lorraine Horsley
illustrated by Caroline Jayne Church

The boy,

the cards,

the presents,

the balloons,

the hats,

the cake.

It is my birthday!

Happy family

written by Catriona Macgregor
illustrated by Sue King

This is my mum.

This is my dad.

This is my sister.

This is my brother.

This is my baby sister.

This is my dog.

This is my family!

Make a cake

written by Marie Birkinshaw
illustrated by Justin Grassi

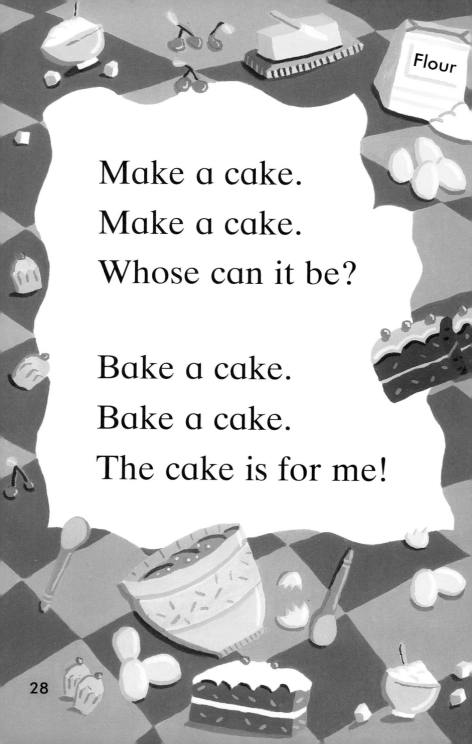

Make a cake.
Make a cake.
Whose can it be?

Bake a cake.
Bake a cake.
The cake is for me!

28

Hop, hop, hop!

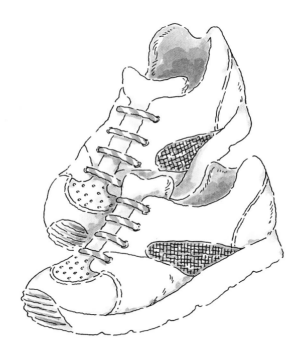

written by Shirley Jackson
illustrated by Annabel Spenceley

Hop,

hop, hop!

Bop,

bop, bop!

Flop,

flop,

FLOP!

Words introduced in this book

birthday   hats   balloons

boy   girl   baby

cake   presents   cards

    a, is, it, my, the, this